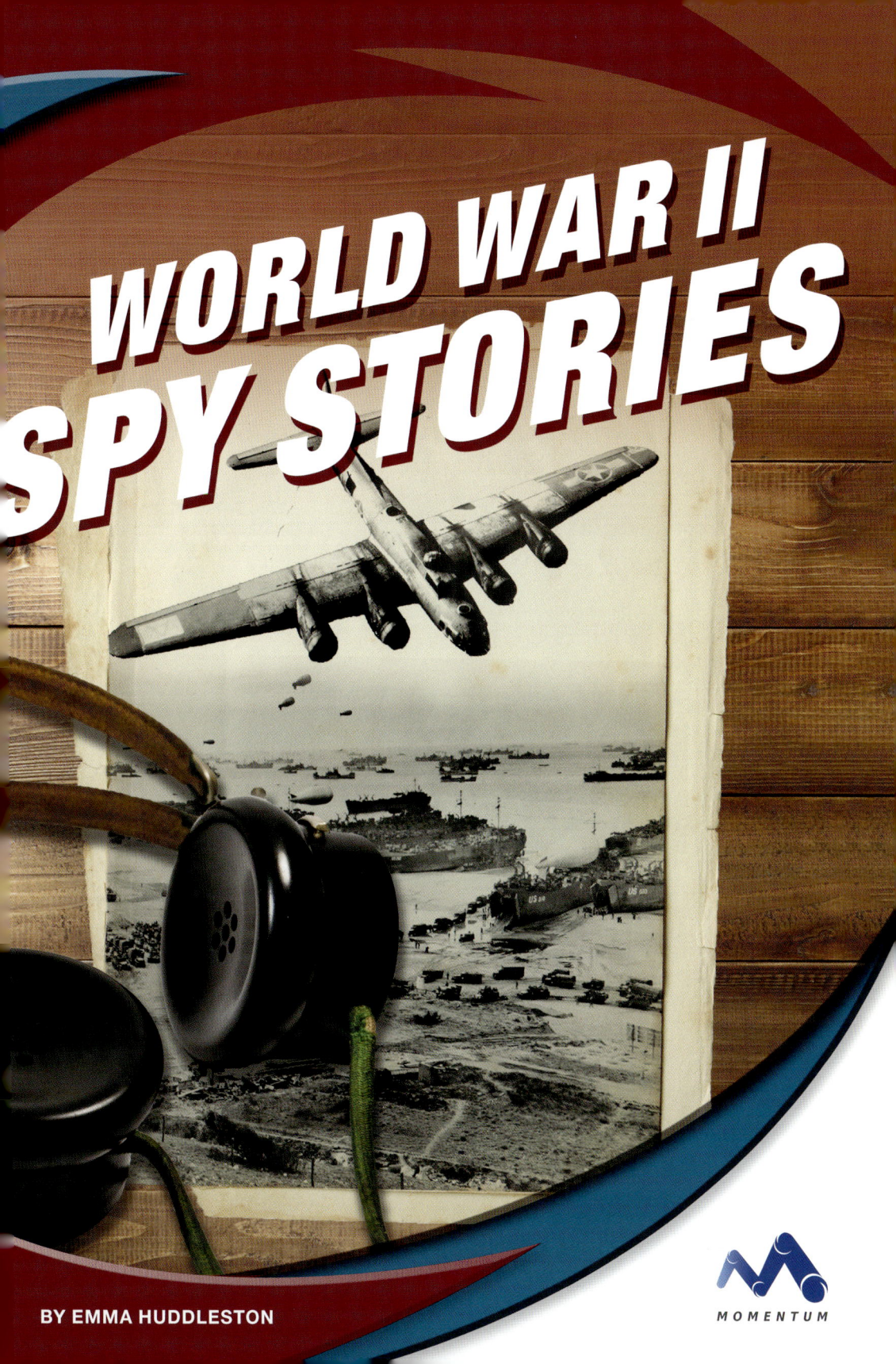

Published by The Child's World®
1980 Lookout Drive • Mankato, MN 56003-1705
800-599-READ • www.childsworld.com

Photographs ©: Everett Historical/Shutterstock Images, cover (plane), cover (boat landing), 1 (plane), 1 (boat landing), 5, 12, 16, 19, 20; Shutterstock Images, cover (wood background), cover (paper), 1 (wood background), 1 (paper); Ralf Siemieniec/Shutterstock Images, cover (headphones), 1 (headphones); AP Images, 6, 8, 14, 18, 25, 28; Berliner Verlag/Archiv/picture-alliance/dpa/AP Images, 10; Peter Hermes Furian/Shutterstock Images, 22; Kirsty Wigglesworth/PA Images/Alamy, 23; dpa/picture-alliance/dpa/AP Images, 24; Bettmann/Getty Images, 26

Copyright © 2021 by The Child's World®
All rights reserved. No part of this book may be reproduced or utilized in any form or by any means without written permission from the publisher.

ISBN 9781503844827 (Reinforced Library Binding)
ISBN 9781503847316 (Portable Document Format)
ISBN 9781503848504 (Online Multi-user eBook)
LCCN 2020931875

Printed in the United States of America

CONTENTS

FAST FACTS 4

CHAPTER ONE
Performer and Spy 7

CHAPTER TWO
Listening through Walls 11

CHAPTER THREE
Counting Ships 15

CHAPTER FOUR
Master of Deception 21

CHAPTER FIVE
Singing for Secrets 27

Think About It   29
Glossary   30
To Learn More   31
Selected Bibliography   31
Index   32
About the Author   32

FAST FACTS

World War II Overview

▶ World War II (1939–1945) started when Germany invaded Poland. Adolf Hitler ruled Germany. His goal was for Germany to take over many areas in Europe. Under Hitler, the **Nazi Party** controlled the country.

▶ Two main groups who fought in the war were the Axis powers and the Allies. The three major Axis powers were Germany, Italy, and Japan. The Allies included France, Britain, the United States, the Soviet Union, and China. Britain and France fought against Germany from the beginning. China was at war with Japan. The Soviet Union and the United States joined the war in 1941.

▶ Hitler commanded a horrific **genocide** of Jewish people, called the Holocaust. Six million Jews were murdered.

▶ World War II was the biggest and deadliest war in history. Some experts estimate that 60 million people may have died.

Spies and Their Tools

▶ Spies had many types of roles. Some got information about the enemy. Others tried to solve coded messages, and some spies went on missions to get information or lead attacks.

▲ **The United States fought in both Europe and the Pacific (pictured) during the war.**

▶ Tools helped spies work secretly. Some weapons for spies were disguised. For example, a pipe pistol was invented for British spies. It blended into a crowd because many people smoked pipes at that time.

▶ Some baby carriages, purses, and violin cases had secret compartments. They could carry radios, weapons, or bomb materials.

▶ People sent hidden messages in many ways. They could roll up tiny pieces of paper and put them into the hollow metal spikes of a fence. They could also use codes or invisible ink.

CHAPTER ONE

PERFORMER AND SPY

Early in the war, celebrity and entertainer Josephine Baker attended many parties throughout Europe. She chatted with military and political leaders. Her bright smile and laugh made it seem like she was just there for fun. But Baker was on a mission. She spied for the French. She tried to find out information by listening to Axis leaders talk. At one point, Baker excused herself. She went to the bathroom. She quickly wrote what she heard on a scrap of paper and hid it beneath her clothes. Then, she put on a big smile and returned to the party. Later, Baker would pass on the information. She could easily carry hidden messages as she traveled to perform.

Baker was an African American who was born in Saint Louis, Missouri. She started her career as a dancer. Later, she became a singer and actress, too.

◀ **Josephine Baker wanted to help France during World War II.**

▲ Baker had a successful career both before and after the war.

Baker moved to Paris at age 19 to perform there. She quickly became a French celebrity during the 1920s.

Baker started spying in 1939. French captain Jacques Abtey had invited her to join the French **resistance** movement. The French resistance worked undercover against the Nazis in German-controlled areas. Spying would be dangerous if she was caught, but Baker agreed right away.

Once Nazi Germany controlled northern France in 1940, Baker had to move. The unfair Nazi rules would **persecute** people who weren't white. Baker went to southern France. Then, she moved to North Africa in 1941. Abtey came with her. They hid information for the French resistance in Baker's sheet music. They wrote between the lines with invisible ink.

In Africa, Baker mainly performed for Allied soldiers. But she continued to help the resistance movement. Her home in southern France was used by agents traveling on missions. Jewish refugees and weapons were also hidden there. After the war, Baker was awarded military honors from the French government.

A RESISTANCE SPY: NANCY WAKE

Nancy Wake grew up in Australia. When the war began, she was living in France. She became a messenger for the French resistance. She passed messages from one spy to another. But Wake was being watched. Germans read her mail and listened to her phone calls. At one point, they offered a large sum of money for her capture. Wake made it through the war and was awarded honors by England and the United States.

CHAPTER TWO

LISTENING THROUGH WALLS

Eric Mark adjusted his headphones. He sat in the basement of Trent Park **estate** in London, England. Mark was listening carefully. On the floors above him, German officers talked. They were prisoners at Trent Park, but they were treated like guests. Comfortable prisoners sometimes spilled secrets about German military plans to each other. They didn't realize that recording devices were hidden in every room. The devices were connected to the basement, where several men were secretly listening. Once Mark heard a German man start talking about an important topic, he began recording the conversation.

Mark was born in Germany. But his parents sent him to England at age 12 because they were Jewish. Nazi laws persecuted Jewish people for their faith, and Mark's parents wanted to keep him safe.

◂ **Adolf Hitler gave many speeches to his supporters. The Allied powers were determined to beat him and Nazi Germany.**

▲ **Concentration camps are sometimes called Nazi death camps. People imprisoned at the camps were frequently tortured, starved, and killed.**

During the war, Mark's parents were sent to a **concentration camp**. Many people who the Nazis didn't like were murdered at such camps. At the time, Mark didn't know whether his parents were alive or dead.

Since Mark could speak both English and German, he was well suited to spy at Trent Park. But working there was not easy. Sometimes, Mark had to act like a waiter or maintenance worker so the Germans wouldn't be suspicious of him being at the estate.

Whenever Mark had to be in the same room as the prisoners, his emotions rose. He fought to keep a straight face when they bragged about the German army's horrible attacks.

Some days, Mark listened for hours and heard nothing important. But one day, he heard a few Germans talking about rockets. He quickly started recording. He learned the location of the weapons. That information was very valuable, and Mark passed it to other agents on his team. They sent reports to the British government and military.

Spies like Mark recorded more than 100,000 conversations. They learned more about Germany's military, weapons, and developing technology. At one point, 59 German generals were held at Trent Park. Mark was one of 100 secret listeners who spied on the German officials and heard them spill military secrets.

SPECIAL OPERATIONS EXECUTIVE

The Special Operations Executive (SOE) was a British agency that had spies in most parts of Europe during the war. Spies watched enemy activity. They also helped resistance groups get supplies or work against Nazi Germany.

CHAPTER THREE

COUNTING SHIPS

During the early years of the war, Bernard Julius Otto Kuehn (nicknamed Otto) prepared to go on a walk past Pearl Harbor in Hawaii. His young son was dressed in a sailor's suit, and the two of them looked like an innocent pair. But as they smiled and looked at the U.S. warships, Otto was spying for the Axis powers. He counted the ships. He memorized their names and locations. Later, he would give the information to Japanese officials living in Honolulu, Hawaii.

Otto joined the Nazi Party in 1930. He and his family moved from Germany to Hawaii in 1935 to spy on the U.S. Pacific Fleet. For years, U.S. officials were suspicious of Otto. He had obvious connections to Japanese and German people. He threw large parties and owned more than one home, but the way Otto made so much money was unclear.

◄ **The USS *Oklahoma* was one battleship in Pearl Harbor.**

▲ Pearl Harbor was a base for the U.S. Navy. Japan wanted to attack it. That way, the United States would have trouble stopping Japan from controlling more areas in Asia.

Secretly, Otto's family was receiving large amounts of money from the Axis powers to spy. However, at the time, U.S. officials didn't have enough evidence to arrest Otto.

In late November 1941, Otto set down his pen. He had finished writing details about the U.S. Pacific Fleet. He planned to sell the stack of papers to Japanese officials. He knew the information would help the Japanese military plan an attack on the U.S. base.

On December 7, 1941, Japan attacked Pearl Harbor. Hundreds of planes flew across the sky. They damaged U.S. ships and planes at the naval base. More than 2,400 Americans died. The attack was a surprise. After Pearl Harbor, President Franklin D. Roosevelt declared war on Japan. The United States was officially in World War II.

After the attack, Japanese officials were found burning stacks of paper. Police arrived and stopped them just in time.

DUQUESNE SPY RING

Many spies gathered information and passed it on through a network. During the war, Fredrick Joubert Duquesne led an Axis spy ring in New York. The network had more than 30 agents. They got information about bombs being made in the United States. However, one member was a **double agent**. William Sebold focused on helping the United States find enemy spies. With Sebold's help, the Duquesne spy ring was uncovered, investigated, and brought to justice.

▲ The U.S. Pacific Fleet had almost 100 ships. Many were damaged in the Japanese attack.

They saved and investigated some papers. The handwritten notes explained details about U.S. Pacific Fleet movements. More evidence pointed to Otto, and he was arrested. Otto confessed to selling intelligence. He was sentenced to 50 years of hard labor instead of death. Later, he and his family were sent back to Germany.

◀ Many U.S. military planes were destroyed in the attack.

CHAPTER FOUR

MASTER OF DECEPTION

In 1941, Juan Pujol cut the end of a tube of toothpaste and squeezed the contents into the trash. Then, he tightly folded a wad of money and put it into a small rubber case. Pujol pushed the case into the empty toothpaste tube and folded the end of the tube to make it look half used. At the airport in Madrid, Spain, security workers didn't question him. They didn't guess the tube was holding thousands of dollars.

Spain supported the Axis powers but did not fight battles in the war. In Madrid, Pujol had secretly met with a group of Nazis. He acted like a Spanish official who was traveling to London. Pujol offered to be a spy for them while he was there. The Nazis accepted his deal. They trained him quickly. They gave him invisible ink, a code book, and money. They had no idea that Pujol planned to be a double agent. Pujol hated Adolf Hitler and the Nazis. He wanted to be a British spy.

◄ **Bomber planes dropped bombs in Europe and the Pacific.**

Instead of going to London, Pujol moved to Lisbon, Portugal. He was nervous to send his first reports to the Nazis. He had to act like he was in London, but he had never been there. He read library books and magazine articles to get facts and details about what life might be like in London. After sending three letters, the Nazis asked for more details about the British military. Pujol was worried. He had no idea how the British military was set up.

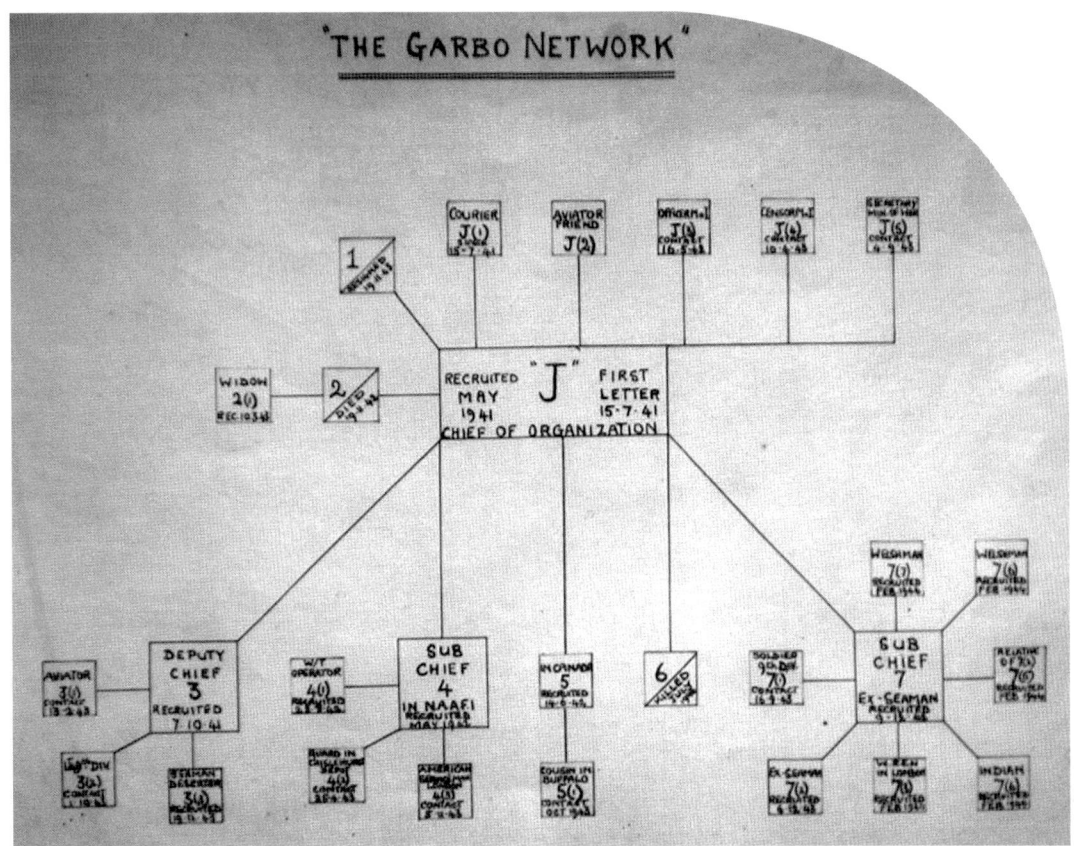

▲ Pujol's spy network was completely fake.

If he didn't prove himself to the Nazis soon, they would consider him useless. Pujol visited a U.S. officer in town. He explained his work and his goal to help the Allies defeat Hitler. The U.S. officer saw how helpful Pujol could be as a double agent. After all, the Nazis trusted him with their code book. So the U.S. officer spoke with British officials and arranged for Pujol to get to London.

The flight to London was cold and crowded. Pujol flew on a small plane. He kept warm by drinking tea. When he arrived, he met with the British agents right away.

▲ **The Normandy invasion marked a turning point in the Allies' favor.**

British agent Tommy Harris was partnered with Pujol. Together, they created Pujol's fake spy network. The Nazis knew Pujol as Agent Garbo. They trusted him and his network so much that they stopped sending other spies to London. They believed Pujol's spies were enough. Now that Pujol was working with British intelligence, he could give better details about military plans. He worked with British officers to lie about troop movements and weapon locations.

By 1944, Allied forces were planning a massive invasion of France, which was held by the Germans. It would take place in Normandy—an area on France's coast. Pujol had to mislead the Nazis in order for the invasion to succeed.

▲ **United States, Canadian, and British troops stormed several beaches in Normandy.**

Before the Normandy attack, Pujol, Harris, and the rest of the spy team convinced the German army of a couple of things. First, they told the Germans to prepare for battle in the wrong location. They got the Germany army to send troops far away from Normandy. Second, Pujol's team misinformed the Germans about the date of the Allied attack. Because of the false information from Pujol, the German army was unprepared. The Battle of Normandy is also known as D-Day. It started on June 6, 1944. The battle was a major loss for Germany and a huge victory for the Allies.

CHAPTER FIVE

SINGING FOR SECRETS

Claire Phillips stepped on stage. A bright spotlight shone on her dress. She faked a smile and began to sing. Men in uniforms and suits sat in the audience. They were Japanese military officers and businesspeople who were visiting her nightclub in Manila, Philippines. They enjoyed food, drinks, and entertainment. Sometimes, they let military secrets slip while talking. When they did, Phillips and her coworkers were there to listen. Phillips was a spy for the Allies.

Phillips was born in Portland, Oregon. In 1941, she traveled to the Philippines. Japan's air force bombed the country while she was there. She and some locals fled to the city of Bataan in the Philippines for safety. Phillips hid in the hills. She saw many wounded people and Allied fighters. She wanted to help.

◀ After the war, Claire Phillips was honored for her work.

▲ U.S. forces battled with the Japanese for control of the Philippines.

One of the Allied commanders asked Phillips to go to Manila and send supplies back. Phillips knew it would be dangerous, but she agreed. Secretly, she sent food and medicine to Filipino and U.S. resistance fighters in Bataan. Phillips earned money through her nightclub, which she opened in 1942. It was located downtown near parks, hotels, and other businesses. It was often packed with people.

At the club, Phillips worked with other young women. They were spies like Phillips. The women had to pretend they agreed with the Japanese guests. Faking agreement was not easy. Sometimes, the Japanese men talked about killing Allied troops. Phillips often felt sad or angered by what she heard, but she kept a smile on her face. She focused on getting more information.

Phillips asked clubgoers questions about where they were going and why. These questions seemed sweet to the men there. But Phillips was looking for details about Axis military plans.

Each day, Phillips met with her coworkers. They talked about what they had heard the night before. They wrote down the names of all the Axis men they could remember. They were lucky if they found out where Axis ships were headed. Then they hid the paper. Messengers delivered it to U.S. and Filipino agents. Some of them rolled the paper up and stuffed it into a hidden compartment in the heel of their shoe. Other times the paper was tucked under the lining of a shopping basket. Phillips's work was stressful. But she knew it was helping the Allied forces. In July 1945, the Philippines were finally free from Japanese control.

THINK ABOUT IT

- Spies could face harsh punishments if caught by the enemy. Why do you think people willingly chose to spy?
- Do you think World War II could have ended differently if neither side had spies? Explain your answer.
- Would you ever consider being a spy or working for a government intelligence agency? Why or why not?

GLOSSARY

concentration camp (kon-shun-TRAY-shun KAMP): A concentration camp was a horrible place where Nazis kept large numbers of people—especially Jewish people—imprisoned, forced them to work, and murdered them. Mark's parents were brought to a concentration camp.

double agent (DUHB-uhl AY-juhnt): A double agent is someone who pretends to be a spy for one side, but he or she is actually loyal to another side. There was a double agent in the spy ring.

estate (eh-STAYT): An estate is a piece of land with a large house on it. Some German prisoners were kept at an English estate.

genocide (JEN-uh-side): A genocide is purposefully destroying a specific race, culture, or political group. The Nazis launched a genocide against Jewish people.

intelligence (in-TEL-i-jence): Intelligence is information about an enemy. Spies passed off their intelligence reports.

Nazi Party (NAHT-see PAHR-tee): The Nazi Party was a political party that governed Germany between 1933 and 1945. The Nazi Party committed horrible crimes against Jewish people.

persecute (PUR-suh-kyoot): Persecute means to harass or cause suffering for a person or group because of their race or beliefs. Baker believed the Nazis would persecute her.

refugees (ref-yoo-JEEZ): Refugees are people who seek safety in a foreign country, especially to avoid war or other dangers. There were many Jewish refugees during World War II.

resistance (ri-ZIS-tenss): Resistance means to work against a group, idea, or leader. The French resistance fought against the Axis powers.

BOOKS

Nicholson, Dorinda Makanaōnalani Stagner. *Remember World War II: Kids Who Survived Tell Their Stories*. Washington, DC: National Geographic, 2015.

Sherman, Jill. *Eyewitness to the Role of Women in World War II*. Mankato, MN: The Child's World, 2016.

Williams, Brian. *World War II: Visual Encyclopedia*. New York, NY: DK Publishing, 2015.

WEBSITES

Visit our website for links about World War II: childsworld.com/links

Note to Parents, Teachers, and Librarians: We routinely verify our Web links to make sure they are safe and active sites. So encourage your readers to check them out!

SELECTED BIBLIOGRAPHY

Cacciottolo, Mario. "The Nazi Prisoners Bugged by Germans." *BBC News*, 18 Jan. 2013, bbc.com. Accessed 15 Oct. 2019.

"Pearl Harbor Spy." *FBI*, n.d., fbi.gov. Accessed 15 Oct. 2019.

"The Secret History of World War II: Spies, Code Breakers, & Covert Operations." *National Geographic*, 5 Oct. 2016, nationalgeographicpartners.com. Accessed 15 Oct. 2019.

INDEX

Baker, Josephine, 7–9

codes, 4–5, 21, 23
concentration camps, 12

Duquesne spy ring, 17

Harris, Tommy, 24–25
Hitler, Adolf, 4, 21, 23
Holocaust, 4

Japan, 4, 15, 17, 27–29

Kuehn, Bernard Julius Otto, 15–17, 19

Mark, Eric, 11–13

Nazi, 4, 8–9, 11–13, 15, 21–24

Pearl Harbor, 15, 17
Phillips, Claire, 27–29
Pujol, Juan, 21–25

recording devices, 11, 13
resistance, 8–9, 13, 28
rockets, 13

Trent Park, 11–13

U.S. Pacific Fleet, 15, 17, 19

Wake, Nancy, 9

ABOUT THE AUTHOR

Emma Huddleston lives in Minnesota with her husband. She enjoys writing children's books and thinks spies are a fascinating part of history!